CW0842768

For Taylor

The Rude Robin © 2019 by Allan Plenderleith
For more books by Allan visit kidstvwriter.com

First published in 2019

by

Ravette Publishing Limited
PO Box 876, Horsham, West Sussex RH12 9GH
www.ravette.co.uk

ISBN: 978-1-84161-413-7

The Rude Robin

by Allan Plenderleith

RAVETTE PUBLISHING

Once upon a Christmas, there was a little robin who was very, very rude.

Thpppppppptptpt!

See what I mean?

She was rude to the postman.

She was rude to the snowman.

She was even rude
to the children.

But this Christmas
her rude ways were
about to change.

It was Christmas Eve and the rude robin saw an old man feeding pigeons in the park.

"Stop feeding those fat pigeons,"
said the rude robin.
"And give me the bread!"

"How rude!" said the old man.
"If you want something
you should say please."

"THPPT! Why are
you feeding pigeons anyway?
They're just greedy!"
said the rude robin.

"Being nice makes me feel good,"
said the old man.
"When you're nice to people,
people are nice to you."

"THPPT! I've never heard such nonsense," said the rude robin. "If you don't believe me, I'll show you!" said the old man.

The old man helped
an old lady across the road.
As he crossed, cars beeped,
trucks honked and
cyclists shouted.

But then the old lady said
"What did you do that for?
I wanted to be on
the other side."

So the old man sighed and
took the lady back across
the road, and as they
crossed, cars beeped, dogs barked,
and cyclists shouted.

The old lady toddled
off grumpily.
"You see," said the rude robin.
"Being nice doesn't get
you anywhere. People are
rude and selfish. THPPPT!"

But the old man was
determined to show
the robin she was wrong.
So he picked a snowdrop and
gave it to a nice lady.

"You see,"
said the rude robin.
"People are horrible!
Best to be horrible back.
THPPPT!"

"Oh no," said the old man. "They can't ALL be horrible. I'll show you." So the old man stood on a park bench and said, "Hello everyone! Isn't today a lovely day?"

But nobody answered. Everyone was rushing around frantically with Christmas shopping bags looking cross.

"We all need to be kind,
every day, but
especially at Christmas.
Being kind makes you feel good!"
said the old man.

Just then a snowball
hit him SPLAT in the face,
and he fell over
onto the bench, breaking it.

A little boy ran off
giggling "HAHA! THPPT!"

"You see," said the rude robin.
"Everyone is rude. THPPPT!"

Just then, the park keeper
plodded up to the old man.
"Oi! You're disturbing
the peace and have caused
destruction to public property.
I'm fining you £50."

And so the poor old man
was given a ticket by
the park keeper.
The rude robin said,
"Now do you believe me –
that everyone is rude
and horrid and selfish?"

"Yes, I think I do,"
said the old man.
"Everyone is rude and
horrid and selfish and it's
time I taught them a lesson."
"What do you mean?"
wondered the rude robin.

The old man took out
his big red mobile phone
and began to
text this message ...

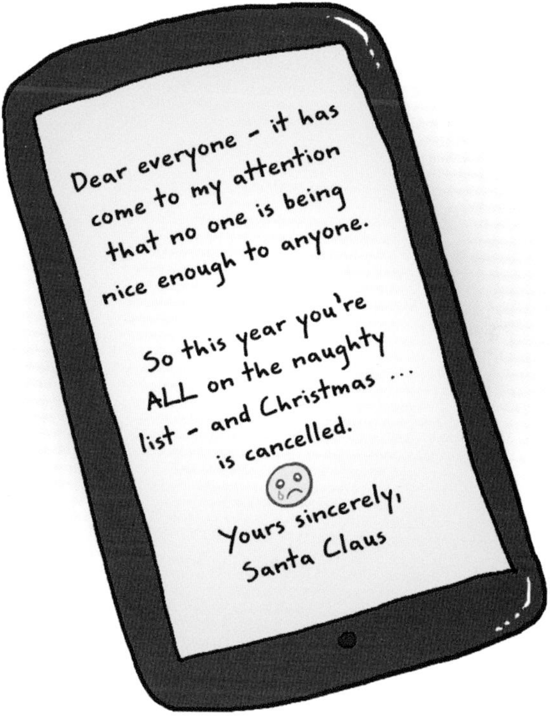
Dear everyone - it has
come to my attention
that no one is being
nice enough to anyone.
So this year you're
ALL on the naughty
list - and Christmas ...
is cancelled.
Yours sincerely,
Santa Claus

"You're Santa Claus?!
Oh no!!" said the shocked robin.

"What have I done!?!"

"I'm sorry," said the rude robin
(for the first time ever).
"I didn't know you were Santa!
You can't give up on everyone!"

"THPPPPT!" said Santa.
"They don't deserve Christmas!
They don't deserve Santa Claus."
Santa sat down on a bench
and began playing
Sweetie Crush Mega Blast
on his phone.

The rude robin felt terrible.
Christmas was cancelled
and it was all her fault.
She had to do something fast!
In a few hours it would
be midnight - Christmas Day!

Then the robin had an idea.
She flew up into the sky,
flying as fast as her
little wings could carry her.

Finally she arrived at the North Pole
(she was a very fast flyer).
She flew through Santa's letterbox
without a moment to lose.

There she found Mrs Claus
who was in the middle
of bingeing on a DVD box set.
"Mrs Claus! Mrs Claus!
It's about Santa!"

Mrs Claus paused the TV and said,
"Santa? Where on earth is he?
He's due at work soon!
Honestly, he only works one day
a year and he's late."

"It's all my fault. I told him everyone was rude and horrid and selfish. But I don't think they really are. I'm sure there must be nice people out there - I just need to prove it!" said the robin.

Mrs Claus thought for a moment.
"Hmm, I think I have an idea."
She produced a small red velvet bag
and whispered into the robin's ear
telling her exactly what to do.

"Thank you," said the robin
(for the first time ever).

So the not-rude-any-more robin
flew back to Santa as fast
as her little wings could carry her.

When she arrived above the city
she sprinkled the contents
all over the houses.

For inside the bag was
Santa's magic dust -
special magic dust to show
what is inside someone's heart.

The magic dust flew into
all the little bedrooms
of all the little sleeping children
and revealed what
was inside their little hearts.

Love!

All the little love hearts flew into
the air and formed a big love heart
in the sky! Santa saw it and realised
that everyone is born kind and full
of love, they just sometimes forget
to show it.

Santa clicked his fingers and
they transported to the North Pole
to give everyone with a
heart full of love,
the best Christmas ever.

The end.

More books by Allan Plenderleith: